Princess Daisy
and the
Dragon
and the
Nincompoop Knights

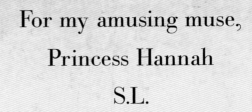

For my amusing muse,
Princess Hannah

S.L.

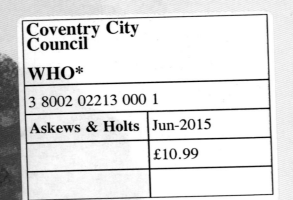

First published in 2015 by Nosy Crow Ltd
The Crow's Nest, 10a Lant Street
London SE1 1QR
www.nosycrow.com

ISBN 978 0 85763 287 6 (HB)
ISBN 978 0 85763 288 3 (PB)

Nosy Crow and associated logos are trademarks and/or
registered trademarks of Nosy Crow Ltd.

A CIP catalogue record for this book is available
from the British Library.

Printed in China
Papers used by Nosy Crow are made from
wood grown in substainable forests.

1 3 5 7 9 8 6 4 2 (HB)
1 3 5 7 9 8 6 4 2 (PB)

Princess Daisy
and the
Dragon
and the
Nincompoop Knights

Written and illustrated by

Steven Lenton

nosy Crow

The trouble with most fairy tales
is that they sound the same.
There's usually a problem
and a **dragon** who's to blame.

And sometimes there's a tower
with a **princess** stuck inside,
a **kingly** dad and lots of **knights**
who often want a bride.

But though this is a fairy tale
with all the usual team,
if you read on you'll find that things
aren't **always** what they seem.

Our story starts at midnight
when the king was gently snoring
and **suddenly** was woken by
some truly **dreadful** roaring.

The townspeople were woken, too.
"Let's go and find the king!
He'll know what to do about
this **terrifying** thing!"

The king was pretty clueless.
"I've hardly slept a wink!"

But Princess Daisy shouted down,
"Hang on, let's have a think!

I can see from way up here
singed trees and a burnt wagon.
The evidence makes me conclude
our problem is a . . .

. . . DRAGON!"

"By Jove, I think you've got it!"
cried the king. "Oh yes! Of course!
And what we need to **fight** it
is a brave knight on a horse."

So the king sent out a message
far and wide across the land,

"Help! We need a hero!
Can you come and lend a hand?"

By Tuesday, three knights had arrived.
They claimed to be the best.
"Just show us where this dragon lives.
We'll rid you of the pest.

And in return we would expect
a princely plot of land,
a bag of gold, a chest of jewels,
oh, and your daughter's hand."

But Daisy shouted to the king,
"Hang on a minute, Dad!
What if we are mistaken
and the dragon isn't bad?

These knights are twits, it's plain to see.
But I know what to do.
If only I weren't in this tower!
Please let me ride out, too!"

"Not a chance!" the king replied.
"It's just not safe," he said.
"Princesses are not
meant to fight.
Now, go and sew
instead."

The knights rode out next morning, with a noisy trumpet blast.
They preened and fluffed their feathers and they **boasted** to the last.

The **first** knight was **Sir Daring-do.** "I'm **fearless, bold** and **brave.**
Just watch me slay the dragon when I ride into that cave."

He galloped up, his sword held high,
and took one look inside . . .
but his legs just turned to jelly.
"Eek! I want my mum!" he cried.

Sir **Musclebound** was next in line. His armour clanked and clinked.
"Forget about Sir Daring-do, he was the **weakest** link.

Look, what you need is **power** and **might**, and I am just your man.
I'll **squash** that dragon in its cave. It's such a simple plan.

You'll be amazed at my great strength.
Just watch me throw this boulder . . .
ouch, **oh no**, I can't go on.
I've really hurt my shoulder."

"Those two knights were no good at all," Sir Brainbox sneered and scoffed.
"I've made a foolproof, fiendish trap." He whipped the cover off.

Sir Brainbox tiptoed to the cave. "Come out, you fiend," he said.
"I've got a kitten sandwich on some pumpernickel bread."

A jet of smoke came from the cave.
He backed towards the trap.
The shiny teeth were ready
and they bit his **bottom** . . .

. . . SNAP!

The king's mouth dropped wide open.
"Oh, who will save us **now**?

But wait!
Here comes
another knight,
who's sitting
on a . . .

. . . COW!"

The people laughed and pointed.

"That armour is a fright."

"He's got a book!"

"He's got no sword!"

"He's far too small to fight!"

"Just watch and learn!"
the knight replied
and rode into the cave.
The crowd all
gasped in horror,
"Who'd have thought
he'd be so **brave?**"

"And then it all went quie[t]
There was not a single soun[d]
"I cannot bear it!" cried the king
and fainted to the groun[d]

The knight was gone for ages
and everyone got bored.
Then, just as it was time for tea,
the dreadful dragon . . .

... SNORED!?

Then, with the dragon sound asleep,
the knight came from the cave
and said, "Don't worry! We're all safe!!"
and gave a cheerful wave.

"This dragon's just a baby!
Come here and take a look.
All she wanted was some milk,
a cuddle and a book."

"And as for all you **nincompoops**,
you **vain** and **foolish** knights,
with all your noise and silliness,
you gave her quite a **fright!**"

"I **know** that voice," the king cried out.
"At least, I **think** I'm right . . .
Daisy, is that you, my dear?
Are **you** our mystery knight?"

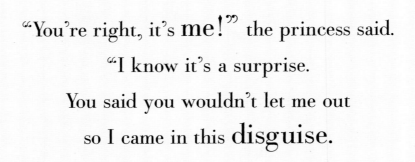

"You're right, it's **me!**" the princess said.
"I know it's a surprise.
You said you wouldn't let me out
so I came in this **disguise**.

I know you put me in a tower
to keep me safe from harm,
but princesses can do **much** more
than curtsey, dance and charm.

Girls are clever, tough and bold
and brave and strong and true.
We're just as good as boys, you know.
We can be heroes, too."

Then everybody cheered, "Well, that's a turn-up for the books!
And doesn't it just go to show you mustn't judge on looks?"

Much later when Queen Daisy ruled,

she kept her dragon friend,

and as they should in stories . . .

. . . they lived happily.

THE END